This book belongs to

....

This edition published by Parragon Books Ltd in 2016 and distributed by

Parragon Inc.
440 Park Avenue South, 13th Floor
New York, NY 10016
www.parragon.com

ISBN 978-1-4748-3879-5

Printed in China

Dory's Ocean Secrets

Bath • New York • Cologne • Melbourne • Delhi
Hong Kong • Shenzhen • Singapore

Fishy Friends

Marlin and Nemo are Dory's best friends. On her journey to the Marine Life Institute, Dory makes lots of new friends—and bumps into some old friends, too. Read about all of Dory's friends below!

Names: Marlin and Nemo
Species: Clownfish

Dory once helped Marlin find his son, Nemo. They traveled across the ocean together, and have been the best of friends ever since! Marlin and Nemo are always there for Dory when she needs them.

Name: Destiny
Species: Whale shark
(but she prefers to be called a whale!)

Destiny was friends with Dory when she lived in the Marine Life Institute. She taught Dory to speak whale!

Name: Bailey
Species: Beluga whale

Bailey is in the Marine Life Institute because he injured his head. He and Destiny are good friends— even if they do argue a lot!

Name: Hank
Species: "Septopus"
(an octopus with only seven tentacles!)

All Hank wants is to live in an aquarium by himself. He might seem cranky, but deep down he's really kind.

Which one of the creatures from the Marine Life Institute would be your best friend?

I would be best friends with..

because ....

....

....

All About You!

Dory is a blue tang. She likes swimming and singing, and she's good at helping others. Dory has short-term memory loss—that's one of the things that makes her so special!

Paste in a photo or draw a picture of yourself here!

Hi, I'm Dory!

Now let's learn all about you!

Name: ....

Age: ....

Birthday: ....

Hair color: ....

Eye color: ....

Height: ....

Something that I'm good at is: ....

....

Something that I like doing is: ....

....

....

Something that makes me special is: ....

....

....

Family Fun

Dory wants to learn more about her family and where she comes from. Tell Dory all about your family!

Parents' names: ....

Brothers' and sisters' names:

....

Who is the oldest? ....

Who is the youngest? ....

Do you have any pets? ....

Who gives the best hugs? ....

Who cooks the best meals? ....

Who is the most forgetful? ....

How would your family describe you?

....

Dory can't really remember what her parents look like . . .
but she thinks they might be blue and yellow! Draw or paste in
a picture of your family below, then label it with their names.

Circle the words that best describe your family!

Large   **Happy**   **Noisy**

Small   **Fun**   **Smart**

Helpful   **Talented**

Dory meets lots of very different ocean creatures during her journey to the Marine Life Institute. Read the info below, and then create a fact file for your friends.

Ocean Fact File

Species: Beluga whale
Fun Fact: Beluga whales can echolocate—that means they use sound to "see" things that are far away.

Species: Whale shark
Fun Fact: Whale sharks are the largest fish in the ocean, and can grow up to 39 feet long!

Species: Octopus
Fun Fact: Octopuses have three hearts and eight tentacles . . . but Hank has only seven tentacles, which makes him a septopus!

Include facts that make your friends special and different—like their best talent or favorite movie!

Friend 1

Name: ....

Fun Fact: ....

....

....

Friend 2

Name: ....

Fun Fact: ....

....

....

Friend 3

Name: ....

Fun Fact: ....

....

....

Dory's Dreams

Dory dreams of being reunited with her family and learning more about her past. What do you dream of? Check off your answers.

Dream Job:
- ○ Astronaut
- ○ Dancer
- ○ Police officer
- ○ Chef
- ○ Doctor
- ○ Artist

Something else: ....

Dream Vacation:
- ○ California
- ○ New York
- ○ Paris
- ○ London
- ○ Tokyo
- ○ Sydney

Somewhere else: ....

Dream Home:
- ○ Castle
- ○ Igloo
- ○ Haunted house
- ○ Mansion
- ○ Spaceship
- ○ Cave

Something else: ....

Write down your biggest dreams, hopes, and wishes here.

....

....

....

....

....

....

....

....

....

....

....

....

....

....

Remember, dreams can be big or small—what matters is that they belong to you!

Ocean Adventure

Dory has to go on a big journey across the ocean to find her family.
She rides on a sea turtle's back and gets chased by a giant squid!
Have you ever gone on a big journey? Write about it here.

Where did you go? ....

How did you travel?

- ◯ Plane
- ◯ Bus
- ◯ Boat
- ◯ Bike
- ◯ Train
- ◯ Car
- ◯ Helicopter
- ◯ On foot

Who did you go with? ....

How long did it take? ....

What was the most exciting part?

....

....

How did it make you feel?

- ◯ Excited
- ◯ Happy
- ◯ Homesick
- ◯ Nervous
- ◯ Tired
- ◯ Hungry

Now imagine that you could go anywhere in the world.
Write about your amazing journey here! Don't forget to include
how you would get there and who you would take with you.

Let your imagination run wild!

....

....

....

....

....

....

....

....

....

....

....

....

....

Magical Memories

Dory has short-term memory loss—but she remembers important things in her own special way. Share your favorite memories with Dory by writing them down below!

My happiest memory is: ....
....
....
....
....

My funniest memory is: ....
....
....
....
....

My earliest memory is: ....
....
....
....
....

Paste in a photo of a happy memory here!

Write down a memory that someone has of you when you were small! It could be a parent, grandparent, or a big brother or sister.

....

....

....

....

....

....

Are you sensible and cautious, like Marlin?
Fearless and adventurous, like Dory?
Or quiet and chilled out, like Hank?
Take the quiz below to find out who
you have most in common with!

Aquatic Quiz

1. What is your favorite color to wear?

a. Orange **b.** Blue **c.** I look good in every color!

2. You are going on a big trip with your family. You feel . . .

a. A bit nervous **b.** Super excited! **c.** I'd rather stay home

3. What is your favorite thing about yourself?

a. I am caring **b.** I am brave **c.** I have a special talent

4. What kind of people do you like to hang out with?

a. Adventurous people **b.** Kind people **c.** Helpful people

5. What are you afraid of?

a. Sharks! **b.** Getting lost **c.** Bullies

Mostly A's
You're most like Marlin!

You are very sensible and practical, and you always look out for the people you love.

Mostly B's
You're most like Dory!

You love fun and adventure, and you have lots of energy! You are always the life of the party.

Mostly C's
You're most like Hank!

You like peace and quiet. You're happy to chill out by yourself—but you're always there for your friends when they need you.

Dream Diary

Dory has dreams about going home. She even tries to swim home in her sleep! What do you dream about? Fill in this dream diary so you can remember.

Date: ....

What my dream was about:

....

....

....

....

....

Date: ....

What my dream was about:

....

....

....

....

Date: ....

What my dream was about:

....

....

....

....

Date: ....

What my dream was about:

....

....

....

....

Date: ....

What my dream was about:

....

....

....

Ocean Animals

What marine creature would you like to be? Circle your favorite in the list below or write something different at the bottom of the page.

Clownfish

Sea lion

Dolphin

Whale

Crab

Shark

Stingray

Giant squid

Octopus

Sea otter

I would like to be a

Draw a picture of yourself as your favorite sea creature here!

Hank is a master of disguise, Bailey can echolocate, and Destiny speaks whale! If you could have any special ability, what would it be?

I would be able to ....

....

....

....

Memory Keeper

Dory forgets easily, which means that things can sometimes get very confusing! Use the spaces below to write down the special things you want to remember—it could be a joke someone told you, a friend's birthday, or something funny that happened to you. Now you'll never forget!

Things I want to remember: ....

....

....

....

....

Things I want to remember: ....

....

....

....

....

Things I want to remember: ....
....
....
....
....

Use this space to doodle any memories you want to keep.

Helping Fins

Best friends like Dory and Nemo always help each other out. Who would you ask to help you out in the following situations?

You can't solve a problem in your math homework.

I would ask .... for help.

You need to buy someone a present.

I would ask .... for help.

You're stuck on a level of a computer game.

I would ask .... for help.

You need to plan a trip.

I would ask .... for help.

You want to bake a birthday cake.

I would ask .... for help.

Marlin and Nemo do everything they can to help Dory get to the Marine Life Institute to find her family. Write about a time when a friend helped you solve a problem or find something important.

....

....

....

....

....

....

....

....

....

....

....

....

....

Dory finds out that she was born in the Open Ocean exhibit in the Marine Life Institute. She lived in a coral cave with her parents, Jenny and Charlie. Now tell Dory all about your home. . . .

Home Sweet Home

Do you have your own bedroom or do you share?

◯ Own room   ◯ Shared room

Do you have a yard?

◯ Yes   ◯ No

Do you have neighbors?

◯ Yes   ◯ No

Describe your home:

....

....

Decribe your bedroom:

....

....

What's your favorite part of your home?

....

....

Paste in a photo or draw a picture of your home here!

Top Talents

Dory has some truly talented and skillful friends to help her on her journey! Hank has camouflage capabilities and is an awesome escape artist, Bailey can use sound to see things far away, and Destiny speaks whale. Look at all the talents listed below and choose one for each of your friends!

Gardening

Juggling

Sign language

Magic

Drawing

Problem solving

Bakir g

Storytelling

Sports

Writing

Playing an instrument

Singing

Swimming

Telling jokes

Acting

Dancing

Math

Friend 1

Name: ....

Talent: ....

Friend 2

Name: ....

Talent: ....

Friend 3

Name: ....

Talent: ....

Friend 4

Name: ....

Talent: ....

Friend 5

Name: ....

Talent: ....

What talent would your friends pick for you?

My talent: ....

....

Tropical fish often have eye-catching markings and colors. Dory is blue with yellow patches, and Marlin and Nemo have orange and white stripes. What are your favorite colors and patterns?

Style Files

Color in the bubbles to show your five fave color combos:

and

and

and

and

and

Check the patterns that you like best:

◯ Spots

◯ Stripes

◯ Swirls

◯ Hearts

◯ Animal print

◯ Checkered

Now try out some of your fave patterns and color combos on these tropical fish!

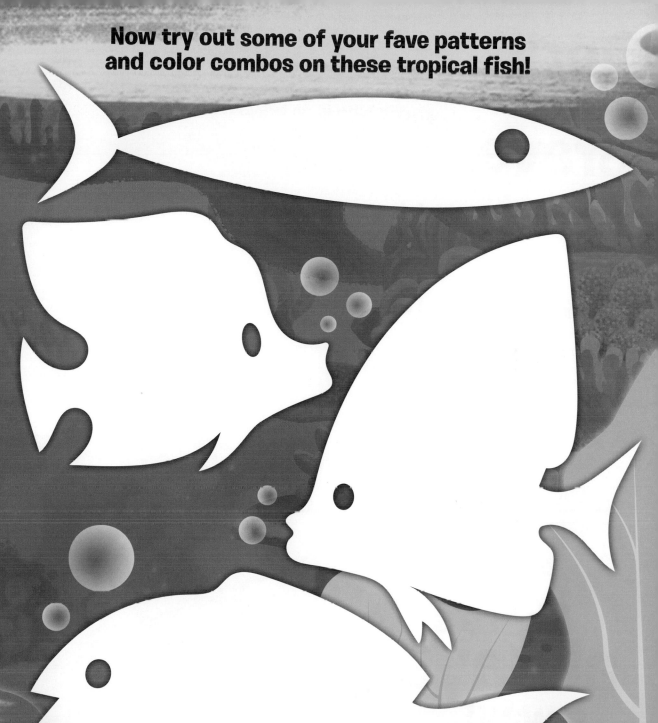

Dory the Brave

Dory might be a little fish, but she has a big heart. She never hesitates to help her friends or other fish in need, and she is very brave. Do you know anyone who is as brave as Dory?

Someone who I think is really brave is

....
....

I think they're brave because

....
....
....

Just stay **calm.**

There's **always** a way!

There **has** to be a way.

Think of a time when you were brave and write all about it here.
Then the next time you feel scared, you can look back at what
you've written and remember how brave you really are!

A time when I was really brave was

....

....

....

....

....

....

....

....

....

....

....

....

Say What?

Destiny speaks whale, and she taught Dory how to speak it, too. What languages do you speak, and what languages would you like to learn?

Check the languages you can speak, and circle the ones you would like to learn.

Danish

Portuguese

Japanese

Italian

Spanish

Polish

Swedish

Turkish

Russian

Greek

Romanian

German

Chinese

French

Others: ....

....

40

Trace the letters below to say "hello" in different languages!

Say hello in French: Bonjour

Say hello in Spanish: Hola

Say hello in German: Hallo

Say hello in Italian: Ciao

Because Dory can be a little forgetful, a diary would be really useful for her! Make sure you don't forget any important plans by writing them in this year planner. Fill your days with fun and friendship!

Dory's Diary

January

....

....

....

....

February

....

....

....

....

March

....

....

....

....

April

....
....
....
....

May

....
....
....
....

June

....
....
....
....

July

August

September

October

....

....

....

....

....

November

....

....

....

....

December

....

....

....

....